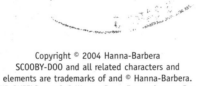

PEUK 0002

Published by Ladybird Books Ltd
A Penguin Company
Penguin Books Ltd, 80 Strand, London, WC2R 0RL, England
Penguin Books Australia Ltd, Camberwell, Victoria, Australia
Penguin Books (NZ) Ltd, Private Bag 102902, NSMC, Auckland, New Zealand

2 4 6 8 10 9 7 5 3 1

Ladybird and the device of a ladybird are trademarks of Ladybird Books Ltd

Manufactured in Italy

www.scoobydoo.com
www.ladybird.co.uk

SCOOBY DOO 2

MONSTERS UNLEASHED

It was a big night for Mystery Inc. They were guests of honour at the opening of Coolsville's National Criminology Museum. The whole town had turned out to see them, and the costumes of the many spooky villains they had put in jail.

A TV journalist called Heather stopped Fred, "May I have a word with Coolsville's hottest detectives?"

"Absolutely!" said Fred.

But Daphne, who didn't like the look of Heather, told Fred they were late and had to get inside.

As they walked into the museum they heard screaming. A costume had come to life! It had belonged to one of their old foes, Dr Jacobo – alias the terrifying Pterodactyl Ghost! He had recently come to a sticky end during an attempt to escape from jail.

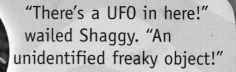

"There's a UFO in here!" wailed Shaggy. "An unidentified freaky object!"

The Pterodactyl Ghost glowed as it snatched up some of the kooky costumes on display. Scooby and Shaggy tried to tie it up – but instead tied themselves to its scaly legs! It dragged them through the air... Luckily, Daphne's neat ninja moves brought them back down to earth – but not before they'd wrecked half the museum!

Suddenly, a masked figure appeared from the shadows. "Revenge is a dish best served cold," he snarled. "Mystery Inc., this time you'll be the ones unmasked – as the buffoons you truly are!"

The gang had work to do.

Mystery Inc. decided to visit one of their old enemies, to see if he knew what was going on. Wickles was the famous Black Knight Ghost but had just been released from jail. The gang sneaked inside his house to look around. Fred, Daphne and Velma found a secret book – HOW TO MAKE A MONSTER!

Meanwhile, Scooby and Shaggy found a note about a secret meeting. "5.30. The Faux Ghost," Shaggy read. "Dude! You found an actual clue!" They decided to investigate their clue – alone!

Right then the dreaded Black Knight Ghost appeared! He was scarily real! The gang only just managed to make their escape with the monster book. They didn't notice the Evil Masked Figure watching from the shadows...

Back at the lab, Velma analysed the pterodactyl scales she had taken from the museum. She found traces of randamonium and looked it up in Wickles' book. "The critical ingredient needed to make a monster!" she gasped.

Randamonium came from silver mines – like the one in nearby Old Coolsville! On the way to check out the mine, the gang passed the Criminology Museum. A big crowd had gathered. There had been another robbery!

Heather told them that more ghosts had stolen all the other spooky costumes! She tricked Fred into seeming stupid, and her cameraman caught it on tape. When her report went out on TV, it made Mystery Inc. look like they didn't care about the safety of Coolsville.

Meanwhile, Scooby and Shaggy had sneaked off to the scary Faux Ghost club, hoping to find more clues. Since it was full of crooks that Mystery Inc. had once sent to prison – including Old Man Wickles – they went in disguise as the famous West Coast Pickleaculas.

"Fifty percent pickles, fifty percent Draculas," explained Shaggy nervously. "One hundred percent terrifying!"

Wickles was taken in by their disguise, and told them all about his life of crime. But when Scooby and Shaggy's disguises slipped off, the crowd turned ugly. The panicking pair had to make a quick getaway – down a rubbish chute!

Wickles left the club soon after. Scooby and Shaggy crept after him – they soon realised he was on his way to the abandoned silver mine...

Fred, Daphne and Velma were already at the mine. They bumped into Wickles and accused him of masterminding a plot to make monsters! But the old man swore he was innocent – he was selling his mine to investors, not digging out randamonium!

Elsewhere in the mine, Shaggy and Scooby wound up in an old elevator. It clunked down slowly, stopping at a creepy old lab. "Like, cluetopia!" cried Shaggy.

They found some potions and, being thirsty, took a sip. It turned them into monsters! Gulping down more gunk in search of a cure, Shaggy grew massive muscles and Scooby turned super-brainy! While Shaggy posed and preened himself, the strange new Scooby got busy with the beakers and whipped up an antidote.

Unfortunately super-muscley Shaggy hurled the antidote away – and it exploded! But as the smoke cleared, Scooby finally cured himself and Shaggy. The rest of the gang arrived to find the explosion had blown a heavy door off the wall – revealing a creepy room on the other side.

Velma found a spooky rhyme on the damaged door: "Beware who enters the monster hive. Inside your fears become alive!"

They had found the secret control room where the mysterious mastermind turned creepy costumes into real-life monsters. But Shaggy and Scooby accidentally set the controls working! A dozen gruesome ghosts popped out of plastic pods in the wall.

"Disconnect that control panel!" Velma snapped. "It'll stop the pods from opening!"

Fred grabbed the control panel. Then, chased by grisly ghosts and skeleton men, Scooby and the gang ran for their lives! They escaped in the Mystery Machine...

Later, they saw Heather again on live TV. "A monster army is tearing Coolsville upside-down in search of Mystery Inc.!" she reported. Then she played a tape sent in by the Evil Masked Figure. "If they don't come back soon," he warned, "your city will be toast!"

"But if we do, he'll get the control panel back," moaned Fred, "and the city will be in even worse shape!"

"The Evil Masked Figure's turning Coolsville into Ghoulsville!" sighed Shaggy.

But luckily, Velma had had a brainwave...

She realised that by reversing the current of the randamonium they could reverse the monster-making process! "All we have to do is rewire this control panel," Velma said excitedly. "We bring it back to the monster hive... "

"We plug it back into the base," Daphne continued, "and all the monsters throughout the city will be destroyed!"

They got to work – but the monsters had found them again! Quickly, the gang piled back into the Mystery Machine for a hair-raising drive to the hive. While Fred battled the Black Knight Ghost, Daphne fought the furious 10,000 Volt Ghost and Velma tackled the Pterodactyl Ghost, Scooby and Shaggy had the most dangerous job of all...

...They had to run with the control panel into the heart of the monsters' lair!

Scooby and Shaggy went so fast that none of the ghosts could keep up with them. "Our years of practice running in fear like lunatics have, like, finally paid off!" puffed Shaggy.

"Yeah-yeah-yeah!" Scooby puffed back.

"Destroy them, my monsters!" cried the Evil Masked Figure desperately.

But it was too late.

With a cry of "Scooby-dooby-dooooooo!" Scooby slapped the control panel into place.

Seconds later Fred, Daphne and Velma caught up with their friends. They watched as the monsters melted messily away! Still, they had managed to capture the Evil Masked Figure.

Huge crowds had gathered in the old mining town. They wanted to see Monster Inc. unmask the Evil Masked Figure. It was Heather, the TV reporter!

"But why did she do it?" asked a reporter.

Daphne pulled off Heather's face – it was a mask! "Because Heather is actually Dr Jonathan Jacobo!"

The truth was out. Jacobo had survived his accident while trying to escape from jail and then come back to Coolsville for revenge on Mystery Inc.! That's why, in disguise as Heather, he tried to turn Coolsville against them – and made it seem like Old Man Wickles was the real monster mastermind!

"And that wraps up another mystery," cried Shaggy. Everyone cheered and clapped – even Wickles!

But no one howled more happily than Scooby, "Rooby-Dooby-Doo!"